Snarky Mom
presents

STOP asking for WATER!

BY ANJEANETTE CARTER

First published in 2021

Written by Anjeanette Carter
Illustrated by Badrus Soleh
Interior design by Bryony van der Merwe

Published by Stratis Corporation

ISBN: 978-1-7376762-0-1 (paperback edition)

For

Wyatt and Everly,

Please go to bed.

Okay honey, it's time to go to bed now.

You've had a long day and you should be tired.

Mommy is very tired and has a lot of Bravo shows to catch up on.

Mom, can I **PLEASE** have some water?

Here's your water.
I filled up your cup just
the way you like it.
No ice.

Thanks, Mom.

Goodnight, honey.

Mom, please can you rub my back before bed?

Okay, honey. Just a quick back rub and then it's off to sleep.

Okay.

Mom?

Yes, honey?

Can you tell me what the weather is going to be tomorrow?

It's going to be 72 and sunny with a slight northwest breeze. Now, goodnight.

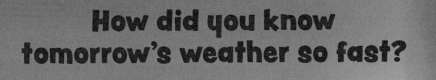

How did you know tomorrow's weather so fast?

Honey, I think you're just stalling now. It's very late and it's time for bed.

You know what? I don't feel like going all the way downstairs to get more water. What if my dragon friend gets it for you?

A dragon?

Yeah, my dragon friend.

You're friends with a dragon?

I sure am.

Hey, Dragon!

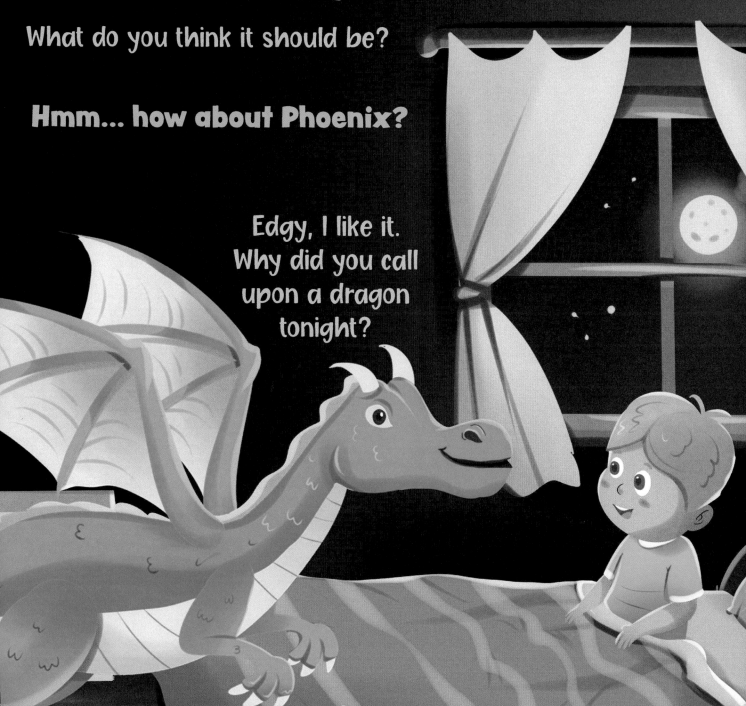

Hey, Dragon!
What's your name?

What do you think it should be?

Hmm... how about Phoenix?

Edgy, I like it.
Why did you call
upon a dragon
tonight?

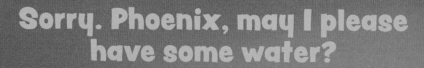

Sorry. Phoenix, may I please
have some water?

That's better.

Here you go. I got it from
the springs of the magical land
where I come from.

Thanks!
Wait, can you
breathe fire?

Sure! I wouldn't
want your water
to be too cold.

Not too cold,
not too hot.

Dragons know
how to make
water just
right.

I think my job here is done. Now, I have to get to another house where the kid won't poop in the potty.

Been there, done that.

Until next time!

Goodbye, Phoenix!

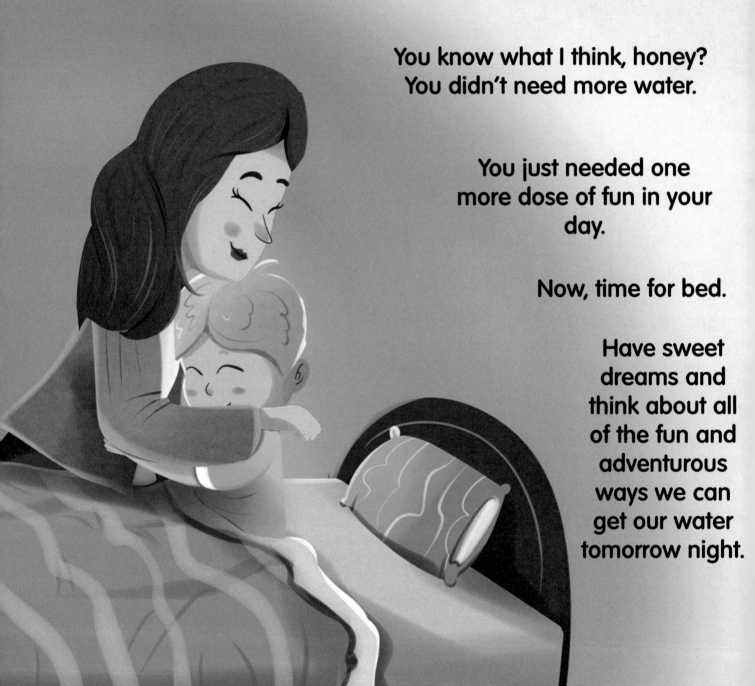

Wow, that was so awesome.

You know what I think, honey?
You didn't need more water.

You just needed one
more dose of fun in your
day.

Now, time for bed.

Have sweet
dreams and
think about all
of the fun and
adventurous
ways we can
get our water
tomorrow night.

Okay, Mommy. Goodnight.

Goodnight, my angel.

Mom?

Yes?

Can I have a pouch?

The End